This book belongs to:

_____

_____

_____

First published by Walker Books Ltd.,
87 Vauxhall Walk, London SE11 5HJ

Copyright © 2014 by Lucy Cousins
Lucy Cousins font copyright © 2014 by Lucy Cousins
Illustrated in the style of Lucy Cousins by King Rollo Films Ltd.

Maisy™. Maisy is a registered trademark of Walker Books Ltd., London.

First U.S. edition 2014

Library of Congress Catalog Card Number 2013944013
ISBN 978-0-7636-7228-7 (hardcover)
ISBN 978-0-7636-7238-6 (paperback)

17 18 19 APS 10 9 8 7 6 5 4 3

Printed in Humen, Dongguan, China.

This book was typeset in Lucy Cousins.
The illustrations were done in gouache.

Candlewick Press
99 Dover Street
Somerville, Massachusetts 02144

visit us at www.candlewick.com

Maisy Plays Soccer

Lucy Cousins

CANDLEWICK PRESS

Good morning, Maisy! What an exciting day! Maisy is going to play soccer. And all her friends are playing, too.

Maisy gets dressed in her special soccer uniform. She ties the laces on her sneakers. Don't forget the ball, Maisy!

Maisy, Cyril, and Eddie are on the red team.

"Go, team!"

It's time to start. The referee blows the whistle—
WHEE!

Maisy is the first to kick the ball....

FOUMPHHH!
Up it goes!

Up, UP, and...
over Cyril's head!

Now Charley
has the ball!

He passes it
to Tallulah....

right into the goal.

Hooray! The blue team has scored a goal.

Everyone is really thirsty from all that running around. They eat some juicy oranges.

Time to get back to the game!
Cyril passes
to Maisy.

Maisy zig-
zags around
Charley.

Talullah tries to steal the ball,

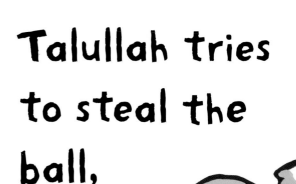

but Maisy kicks it to Cyril.

Wow, Cyril's so *fast*!
He really wants to score
a goal for the red team.
Come on, Cyril!
You can do it!

He runs and runs and gives the
ball one BIG kick into the net . . .
GOOOOOOAL!

WHEEEEEE! The referee blows the whistle. The game is over.

One goal for the red team, and one goal for the blue team. Well done, everybody!

"It's a tie!"

Maisy and her friends love playing soccer. It doesn't matter who wins. It's just lots of fun.